LAUREN CHILD is the creator of the bestselling
Charlie and Lola books, also a children's television animation series.
I Want a Pet is Lauren's very first picture book, celebrating its 15th anniversary in 2014.
Inspired to write *I Want a Pet* after seeing a friend look into a pet shop window,
Lauren was once the proud owner of sixteen guinea pigs, two goldfish,
two hamsters, one tortoise and hundreds of stick insects – all at the same time.

Quarto is the authority on a wide range of topics.

Quarto educates, entertains and enriches the lives of
our readers—enthusiasts and lovers of hands-on living.

www.quartoknows.com

For my mother and father who gave me my first pet Michael (a goldfish)
and ended up with 16 guinea pigs, 2 hamsters and a tortoise

First published in Great Britain in 1999 by
Frances Lincoln Children's Books,
74-77 White Lion Street, London N1 9PF
www.franceslincoln.com

This paperback edition published in 2007

A catalogue record for this book is available from the British Library.

ISBN 978-0-7112-1339-5

Printed and bound by CPI Group (UK) Ltd, Croydon, CR0 4YY

MIX
Paper from
responsible sources
FSC® C013604

I Want a pet

Lauren Child

F

FRANCES LINCOLN

CHILDREN'S BOOKS

I *really* want a pet.

"Please Mum, can I have a pet?"

Mum says, "Well – perhaps something with not too much fur."

Dad says, "Maybe something that lives outside."

Granny says, "Nothing with a buzz." It interferes with her hearing aid.

Grandad says, "Stuffed pets are very reliable."

The pet shop lady says, "Goldfish can be fun."

I say, "How?"

Mum asks, "What sort of pet would you like?"
I say, "How about an African lion? I'd train him
and we could do a show. We'd be a roaring success."

Granny says, "Lions have a habit of snacking between meals."

I think, uh-oh ...

"A sheep would be nice, and they're vegetarian. We could knit jumpers together."

Grandad says, "Sheep are forever following you around. They haven't got minds of their own."

I hate copy-cats.

"How about a wolf? I bet they have lots of good ideas.
And wolves are good sniffers, so we'd never get lost."

Dad says, "Wolves are also good at howling.
Howling gives me a headache."

Dad isn't much fun when he's got a headache.

"Maybe an octopus is the answer. They're quiet, and we could go diving in the bath."

Mum says, "Have you any idea how many footprints an octopus would make?"
I say, "Eight."

Mum says, "Exactly."

"A boa constrictor would be perfect. They don't have legs, and they hardly make a sound."

Dad says, "Boa constrictors have a habit of wrapping themselves around you and squeezing too tightly."

Maybe I want a pet that's a bit less friendly.

"How about a bat? At night we could flap around, and during the day we'd dangle upside-down in the wardrobe."

Mum says, "If anyone mentions bats in the wardrobe, there'll be no chocolate éclairs!"

Chocolate éclairs are my favourite.

So I must try and find a pet that
won't eat me,
won't copy my ideas,
won't make too much noise,

won't leave dirty footprints round the house,
won't squeeze me too hard,
and won't make my mum so cross, she cancels
chocolate éclairs.

The pet shop lady says she can think of one thing that doesn't leave footprints, doesn't eat, doesn't move and doesn't make a squeak.

No one's exactly sure what it is, because it's not quite a pet yet...

but it will be soon.

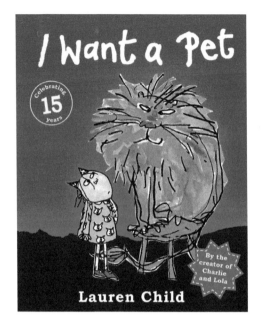

Look out for the miniature hardback edition of *I Want A Pet*,

published in September 2013.

ISBN 978-1-84780-334-4

£4.99

Frances Lincoln children's books are available from all good bookshops.
You can also buy books and find out more about your favourite titles,
authors and illustrators on our website: www.frances-lincoln.com